SPOON

written by

Amy Krouse Rosenthal

illustrated by

Scott Magoon

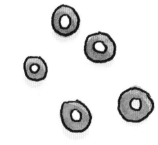

DISNEP • HYPERION BOOKS 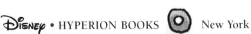 New York

First Edition
10 9 8 7
H106-9333-5-13304

Printed in Malaysia

ISBN 978-1-4231-0685-2

Library of Congress Cataloging-in-Publication Data on file.

Visit www.hyperionbooksforchildren.com

To my spooning partner,
Jason

—A.K.R.

To Alessandra and
Margaret
—S.M.

This is Spoon's family.

On Sundays, Spoon goes to visit his Aunt Silver.
He has to be on his very best behavior there.
She's very fancy and proper.

"Good-bye, darling!
Ta, ta!"

At bedtime, Spoon likes to hear the story about his adventurous great-grandmother, who fell in love with a dish and ran off to a distant land.

Lately, though, Spoon had been feeling blue.

"What's wrong?" asked his mother.
"You look a bit bent out of
shape."

"Nothing," mumbled Spoon.

"It's just that . . . I don't know . . .
All my friends have it so much
better than me.

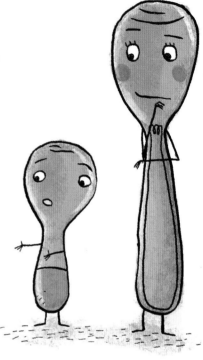

Like Knife.
Knife is so lucky!
He gets to cut,

he gets to spread.
I never get to cut or spread."

"Yes, Knife is pretty spiffy that way, isn't he?"

"And Fork, Fork is so lucky!
She gets to go practically EVERYWHERE.
I bet she never goes stir-crazy like I do."

"Fork does get out and make
herself useful, doesn't she?"

"And Chopsticks! They are so lucky!
Everyone thinks they're really cool and exotic.
No one thinks I'm cool or exotic."

"Those Chopsticks are
something else, aren't they?"

Meanwhile . . . if only Spoon knew what his friends were saying at that very minute!

"Spoon is so lucky!" said Knife. "He's so fun and easygoing. Everyone's so serious with me; no one's ever allowed to be silly with me like they are with Spoon."

"Spoon is so lucky!" said Fork. "He gets to measure stuff. No one ever does that with me."

"Spoon is so lucky!" said Chopsticks.
"He can go places by himself.
We could never function apart."

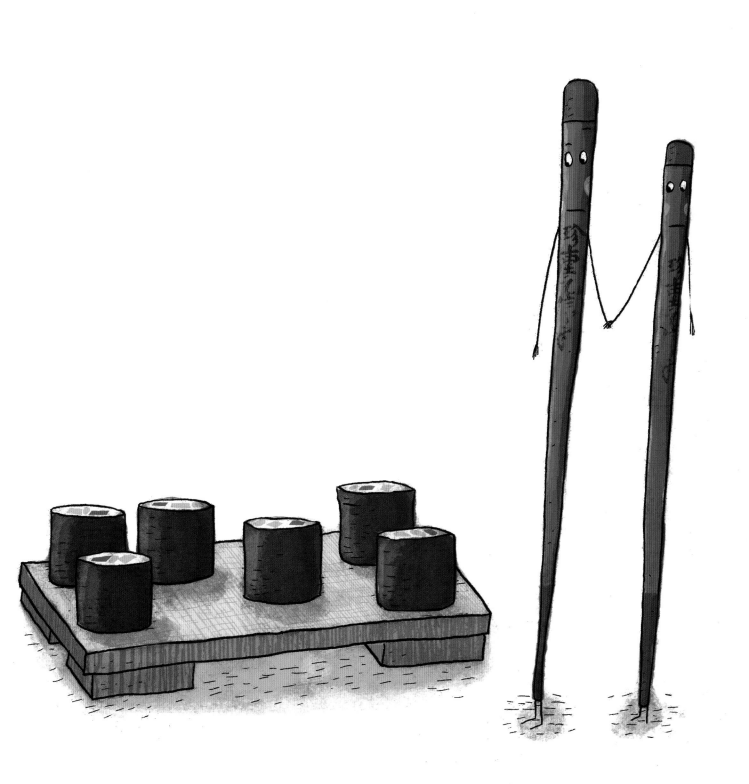

That night after bedtime stories, Spoon's mom turned off the light, tucked him in, and said . . .

"You know, Spoon—I wonder if you realize just how lucky you are.

"Your friends will never know
the joy of diving headfirst
into a bowl of ice cream."

"They'll never know what it feels like to clink against the side of a cereal bowl.

"They'll never be able to twirl around in a mug, or relax in a hot cup of tea."

Spoon hadn't thought of it that way before.
He lay awake in bed for a long time.
His mind was racing . . . he felt so alive!

There was only one thing to do.

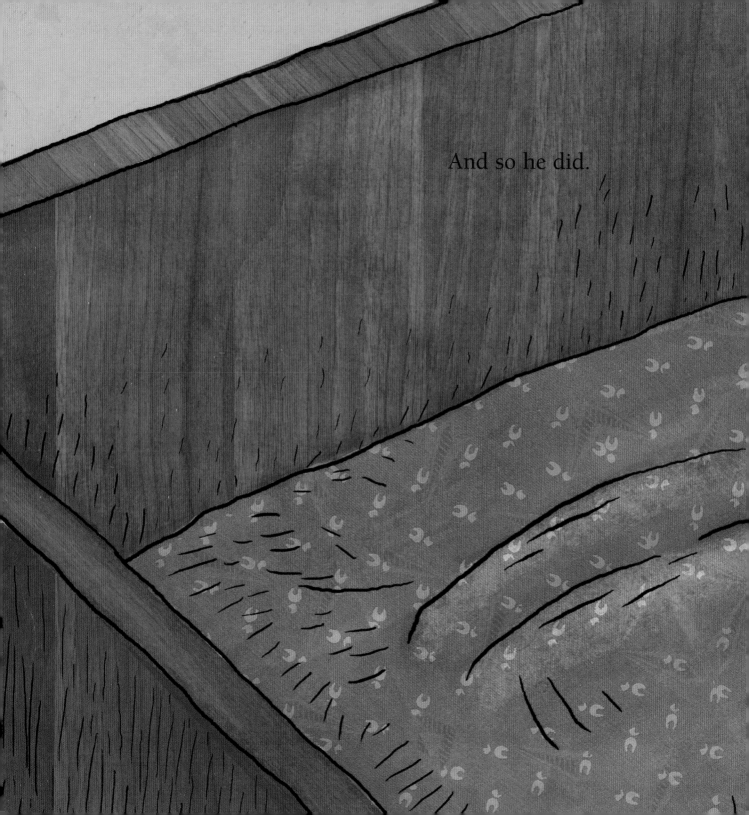

And so he did.

Sweet dreams.